ILLUMINATION PRESENTS

THE SECRET LIFE OF PETS™

MAX AND FRIENDS

Adapted by Dennis R. Shealy • Illustrated by Craig Kellman

SECRET LIFE OF PETS: MAX AND FRIENDS
A CENTUM BOOK 9781910916933
Published in Great Britain by Centum Books Ltd
This edition published 2016
© 2016 Universal Studios LLC.
1 3 5 7 9 10 8 6 4 2
The Secret Life of Pets is a trademark and copyright of Universal Studios. Licensed by Universal Studios Licensing LLC. All rights reserved.

UNIVERSAL
A COMCAST COMPANY

All rights reserved. No part of this publication may be reproduced, stored in a retrieval system, or transmitted in any form or by any mean,
electronic, mechanical, photocopying, recording or otherwise without the prior permission of the publishers.
Centum Books Ltd, 20 Devon Square, Newton Abbot, Devon TQ12 2HR, UK
books@centumbooksltd.co.uk
CENTUM BOOKS Limited Reg. No. 07641486
A CIP catalogue record for this book is available from the British Library
Printed in China.

Hi! My name is Max. I'm the luckiest dog in the whole world. I live in New York City with my owner, Katie. She's the greatest!

Katie and I have a love stronger than words . . .
or even shoes. (And Katie has great taste in shoes!)

It's me and Katie. Katie and me.
US AGAINST THE WORLD.

The only problem is that almost every day she leaves.

I miss Katie very much . . .

. . . but it's not so bad because I have other friends who live in the building. They're pets like me.

GIDGET is my Pomeranian neighbour.
Every day she asks me what my plans are.
I always tell her I'm going to sit and wait for
Katie. Gidget thinks my life is very exciting.

CHLOE is a big grey cat that lives in my building. She's mostly interested in food and can't always be bothered to give advice. As soon as her owner leaves for the day, she . . .

. . . EATS!

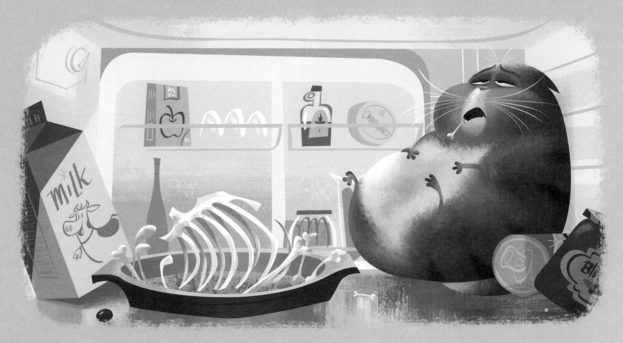

(Perhaps a little too much.)

sweetpea is a bird who likes to dream big.

When his owner is away,
Sweetpea flies into the
DANGER ZONE!

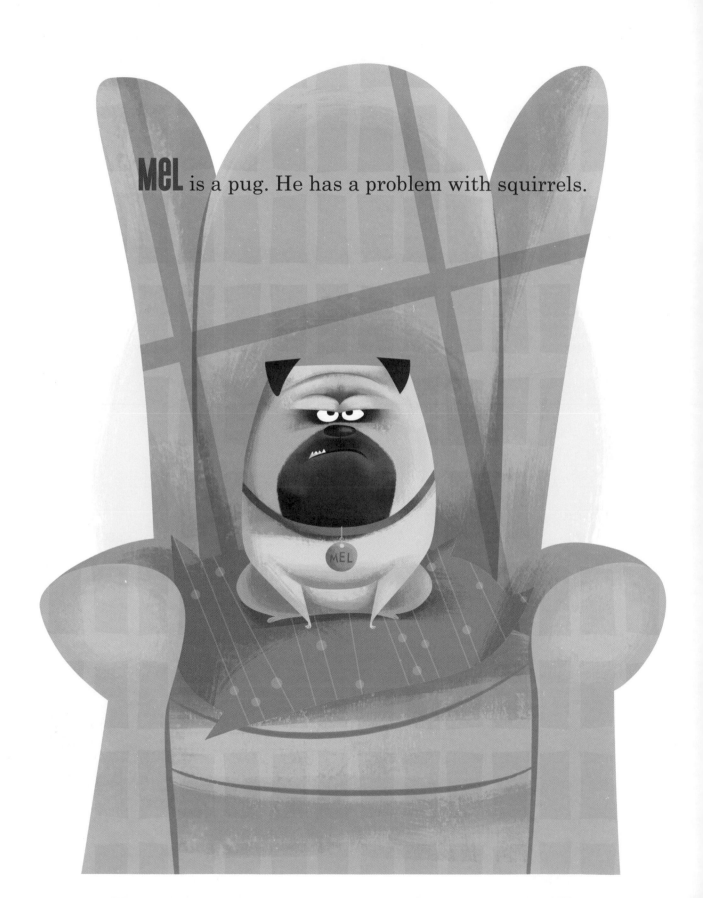

MeL is a pug. He has a problem with squirrels.

He barks to let them know to stay away – this is *his* territory!

LEONARD is a poodle. He may act reserved
when his owner is around . . .

. . . but once he leaves, Leonard likes to let loose and head-bang to his hard-rocking music!

My buddy **BUDDY** is a dachshund who loves being massaged so much that he's found a clever way to work out the kinks in his long back even when his owner isn't home.

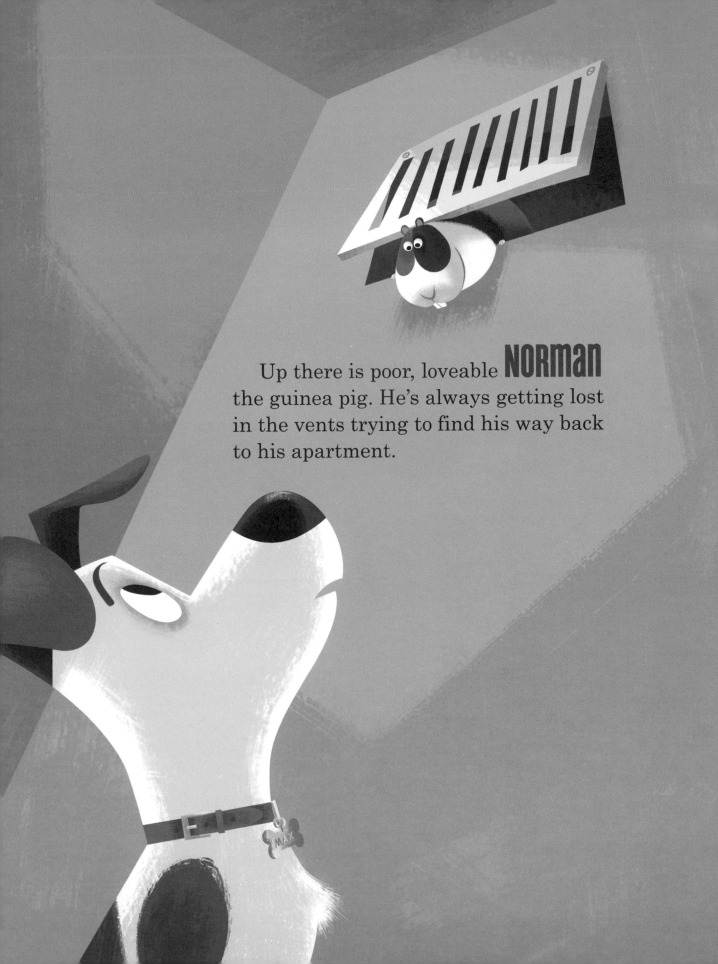

Up there is poor, loveable **NORMAN** the guinea pig. He's always getting lost in the vents trying to find his way back to his apartment.

And then there's **POPS**. Don't worry about the wheels – this old basset hound can still get around. Since his owner is never home, everyone likes to hang out at Pops's place.

Yup. My life is perfect. I get to spend time with my friends, and then it's my favourite part of the day – when Katie comes home and it's just the two of us again.

Hey, here's Katie now!

And she brought me something. She's so great!

It's a . . .

It's a . . .